Close Your Eyes

Jean Marzollo
Close Your Eyes
pictures by Susan Jeffers

Dial Books
for Young Readers
New York

Published by Dial Books for Young Readers
A Division of NAL Penguin Inc.
2 Park Avenue
New York, New York 10016

Published simultaneously in Canada by
Fitzhenry & Whiteside Limited, Toronto

Library of Congress Cataloging in Publication Data
Marzollo, Jean.
Close your eyes.

Summary: A lullaby interspersed with illustrations
of a father's efforts to put his reluctant child to bed.
[1. Lullabies.] I. Jeffers, Susan, ill. II. Title.
PZ8.3.M419C1 [E] 76-42935
ISBN 0-8037-1609-5
ISBN 0-8037-1610-9 lib.bdg.

for David Andre Bates Marzollo
for Little Ernie

Close your eyes and you can be

Sound asleep in an apple tree

Or if you like

on a ship at sea.

Close your eyes and you can play

With woolly lambs on a lazy day

Or tabby cats in a pile of hay.

Close your eyes and you can lie

Hidden deep in a field of rye

Or on a cloud in a sunset sky.

Close your eyes and gently rest

Cuddled on a panda's chest

Or with a friend in a robin's nest.

Close your eyes and with a yawn

Imagine drowsy geese at dawn

Or lightning bugs on a quiet lawn.

But you've not heard a word I've said

For you're asleep in a cozy bed

With secret dreams in your lovely head.

Goodnight.